THE ADVENTURE OF THE DYING DETECTIVE

THE ADVENTURE OF THE DYING DETECTIVE

BY

SIR ARTHUR CONAN DOYLE

KALPAZ

ISBN: 978-93-5128-667-7(HB)

First Published in 1913
Indian Reprint in 2017

Published by

Kalpaz Publications
C-30, Satyawati Nagar,
Delhi – 110052
E-mail: kalpaz@hotmail.com
Website: kalpazpublications.com
Ph.: +91-9212142040

Mrs. Hudson, the landlady of Sherlock Holmes, was a long-su”ering woman. Not only was her ˇrst-oor at invaded at all hours by throngs of singular and often undesirable char- acters but her remarkable lodger showed an eccentricity and irregularity in his life which must have sorely tried her patience. His incredible untidiness, his addiction to music at strange hours, his occasional revolver practice within doors, his weird and often malodorous scientiˇc experiments, and the atmosphere of violence and danger which hung around him made him the very worst tenant in London. On the other hand, his payments were princely. I have no doubt that the house might have been purchased at the price which Holmes paid for his rooms during the years that I was with him.

The landlady stood in the deepest awe of him and never dared to interfere with him, however outrageous his proceedings might seem. She was fond of him, too, for he had a remarkable gentleness and courtesy in his dealings with women. He disliked and distrusted the sex, but he was always a chivalrous opponent. Knowing how genuine was her regard for him, I listened earnestly to her story when she came to my rooms in the second year of my married life and told me of the sad condition to which my poor friend was reduced.

“He’s dying, Dr. Watson,” said she. “For three days he has been sinking, and I doubt if he will last the day. He would not let me get a doctor. This morning when I saw his bones sticking out of his face and his great bright eyes looking at me I could stand no more of it. ‘With your leave or without it, Mr. Holmes, I am going for a doctor this very hour,’ said I. ‘Let it be Watson, then,’ said he. I wouldn’t waste an hour in coming to him, sir, or you may not see him alive.”

I was horriˇed for I had heard nothing of his illness. I need not say that I rushed for my coat and my hat. As we drove back I asked for the details.

“There is little I can tell you, sir. He has been working at a case down at Rotherhithe, in an alley near the river, and he has brought this illness back with him. He took to his bed on Wednesday afternoon and has never moved since. For these three days neither food nor drink has passed his lips.”

“Good God! Why did you not call in a doctor?”

“He wouldn’t have it, sir. You know how masterful he is. I didn’t dare to disobey him.

But he’s not long for this world, as you’ll see for yourself the moment that you set eyes on him.”

He was indeed a deplorable spectacle. In the dim light of a foggy November day the sick room was a gloomy spot, but it was that gaunt, wasted face staring at me from the bed which sent a chill to my heart. His eyes had the brightness of fever, there was a hectic ush upon either cheek, and dark crusts clung to his lips; the thin hands upon the coverlet twitched incessantly, his voice was croaking and spasmodic. He lay listlessly as I entered the room, but the sight of me brought a gleam of recognition to his eyes.

1

"Well, Watson, we seem to have fallen upon evil days," said he in a feeble voice, but with something of his old carelessness of manner.

"My dear fellow!" I cried, approaching him.

"Stand back! Stand right back!" said he with the sharp imperiousness which I had asso- ciated only with moments of crisis. "If you approach me, Watson, I shall order you out of the house."

"But why?"

"Because it is my desire. Is that not enough?"

Yes, Mrs. Hudson was right. He was more masterful than ever. It was pitiful, however, to see his exhaustion.

"I only wished to help," I explained.

"Exactly! You will help best by doing what you are told."

"Certainly, Holmes."

He relaxed the austerity of his manner.

"You are not angry?" he asked, gasping for breath.

Poor devil, how could I be angry when I saw him lying in such a plight before me?

"It's for your own sake, Watson," he croaked.

"For MY sake?"

"I know what is the matter with me. It is a coolie disease from Sumatra{a thing that the Dutch know more about than we, though they have made little of it up to date. One thing only is certain. It is infallibly deadly, and it is horribly contagious."

He spoke now with a feverish energy, the long hands twitching and jerking as he motioned me away.

"Contagious by touch, Watson{that's it, by touch. Keep your distance and all is well."

"Good heavens, Holmes! Do you suppose that such a consideration weighs with me of an instant? It would not a"ect me in the case of a stranger. Do you imagine it would prevent me from doing my duty to so old a friend?"

Again I advanced, but he repulsed me with a look of furious anger.

"If you will stand there I will talk. If you do not you must leave the room."

I have so deep a respect for the extraordinary qualities of Holmes that I have always deferred to his wishes, even when I least understood them. But now all my professional instincts were aroused. Let him be my master elsewhere, I at least was his in a sick room.

"Holmes," said I, "you are not yourself. A sick man is but a child, and so I will treat you. Whether you like it or not, I will examine your symptoms and treat you for them."

He looked at me with venomous eyes.

"If I am to have a doctor whether I will or not, let me at least have someone in whom I have conˇdence," said he.

"Then you have none in me?"

"In your friendship, certainly. But facts are facts, Watson, and, after all, you are only a general practitioner with very limited experience and mediocre qualiˇcations. It is painful to have to say these things, but you leave me no choice."

I was bitterly hurt.

"Such a remark is unworthy of you, Holmes. It shows me very clearly the state of your own nerves. But if you have no conˇdence in me I would not intrude my services. Let me bring Sir Jasper Meek or Penrose Fisher, or any of the best men in London. But someone you MUST have, and that is ˇnal. If you think that I am going to stand here and see you die without either helping you myself or bringing anyone else to help you, then you have mistaken your man."

"You mean well, Watson," said the sick man with something between a sob and a groan.

"Shall I demonstrate your own ignorance? What do you know, pray, of Tapanuli fever?

What do you know of the black Formosa corruption?"

"I have never heard of either."

"There are many problems of disease, many strange pathological possibilities, in the East,

Watson." He paused after each sentence to collect his failing strength. "I have learned so much during some recent researches which have a medico-criminal aspect. It was in the course of them that I contracted this complaint. You can do nothing."

"Possibly not. But I happen to know that Dr. Ainstree, the greatest living authority upon tropical disease, is now in London. All remonstrance is useless, Holmes, I am going this instant to fetch him." I turned resolutely to the door.

Never have I had such a shock! In an instant, with a tiger-spring, the dying man had intercepted me. I heard the sharp snap of a twisted key. The next moment he had staggered back to his bed, exhausted and panting after his one tremendous outame of energy.

"You won't take the key from me by force, Watson, I've got you, my friend. Here you are, and here you will stay until I will otherwise. But I'll humour you." (All this in little gasps, with terrible struggles for breath between.) "You've only my own good at heart. Of course I know that very well. You shall have your way, but give me time to get my strength.

Not now, Watson, not now. It's four o'clock. At six you can go."

"This is insanity, Holmes."

"Only two hours, Watson. I promise you will go at six. Are you content to wait?"

"I seem to have no choice."

"None in the world, Watson. Thank you, I need no help in arranging the clothes. You will please keep your distance. Now, Watson, there is one other condition that I would make.

You will seek help, not from the man you mention, but from the one that I choose."

"By all means."

"The ˇrst three sensible words that you have uttered since you entered this room,Watson.

You will ˇnd some books over there. I am somewhat exhausted; I wonder how a battery feels when it pours electricity into a non-conductor? At six, Watson, we resume our conversation."

But it was destined to be resumed long before that hour, and in circumstances which gave me a shock hardly second to that caused by his spring to the door. I had stood for some minutes looking at the silent ˇgure in the bed. His face was almost covered by the clothes and he appeared to be asleep. Then, unable to settle down to reading, I walked slowly round the room, examining the pictures of celebrated criminals with which every wall was adorned. Finally, in my aimless perambulation, I came to the mantelpiece. A litter of pipes, tobacco-pouches, syringes, penknives, revolver-cartridges, and other debris was scat- tered over it. In the midst of these was a small black and white ivory box with a sliding lid. It was a neat little thing, and I had stretched out my hand to examine it more closely, when|-

It was a dreadful cry that he gave{a yell which might have been heard down the street. My skin went cold and my hair bristled at that horrible scream. As I turned I caught a glimpse of a convulsed face and frantic eyes. I stood paralyzed, with the little box in my hand.

"Put it down! Down, this instant, Watson{this instant, I say!" His head sank back upon the pillow and he gave a deep sigh of relief as I replaced the box upon the mantelpiece. "I hate to have my things touched, Watson. You know that I hate it. You it dget me beyond endurance. You, a doctor you are enough to drive a patient into an asylum. Sit down, man, and let me have my rest!"

The incident left a most unpleasant impression upon my mind. The violent and cause- less excitement, followed by this brutality of speech, so far removed from his usual suavity, showed me how deep was the disorganization of his mind. Of all ruins, that of a noble mind is the most deplorable. I sat in silent dejection until the stipulated time had passed. He seemed to have been watching the clock as well as I, for it was hardly six before he began to talk with the same feverish animation as before.

"Now, Watson," said he. "Have you any change in your pocket?"

"Yes."

"Any silver?"

"A good deal."

"How many half-crowns?"

"I have ˇve."

"Ah, too few! Too few! How very unfortunate, Watson! However, such as they are you can put them in your watchpocket. And all the rest of your money in your left trouser pocket. Thank you. It will balance you so much better like that."

This was raving insanity. He shuddered, and again made a sound between a cough and a sob.

"You will now light the gas, Watson, but you will be very careful that not for one instant shall it be more than half on. I implore you to be careful, Watson. Thank you, that is excellent. No, you need not draw the blind. Now you will have the kindness to place some letters and papers upon this table within my reach. Thank you. Now some of that litter from the mantelpiece. Excellent, Watson! There is a sugar-tongs there. Kindly raise that small ivory box with its assistance. Place it here among the papers. Good! You can now go and fetch Mr. Culverton Smith, of 13 Lower Burke Street."

To tell the truth, my desire to fetch a doctor had somewhat weakened, for poor Holmes was so obviously delirious that it seemed dangerous to leave him. However, he was as eager now to consult the person named as he had been obstinate in refusing.

"I never heard the name," said I.

"Possibly not, my good Watson. It may surprise you to know that the man upon earth who is best versed in this disease is not a medical man, but a planter. Mr. Culverton Smith is a well-known resident of Sumatra, now visiting London. An outbreak of the disease upon his plantation, which was distant from medical aid, caused him to study it himself, with some rather far-reaching consequences. He is a very methodical person, and I did not desire you to start before six, because I was well aware that you would not find him in his study. If you could persuade him to come here and give us the benefit of his unique experience of this disease, the investigation of which has been his dearest hobby, I cannot doubt that he could help me."

I gave Holmes's remarks as a consecutive whole and will not attempt to indicate how they were interrupted by gaspings for breath and those clutchings of his hands which indicated the pain from which he was su"ering. His appearance had changed for the worse during the few hours that I had been with him. Those hectic spots were more pronounced, the eyes shone more brightly out of darker hollows, and a cold sweat glimmered upon his brow. He still retained, however, the jaunty gallantry of his speech. To the last gasp he would always be the master.

"You will tell him exactly how you have left me," said he. "You will convey the very impression which is in your own mind{a dying man{a dying and delirious man. Indeed, I cannot think why the whole bed of the ocean is not one solid mass of oysters, so prolific the creatures seem. Ah, I am wandering! Strange how the brain controls the brain! What was I saying, Watson?"

"My directions for Mr. Culverton Smith."

"Ah, yes, I remember. My life depends upon it. Plead with him, Watson. There is no good feeling between us. His nephew, Watson{I had suspicions of foul play and I allowed him to see it. The boy died horribly. He has a grudge against me. You will soften him, Watson. Beg him, pray him, get him here by any means. He can save me-only he!"

"I will bring him in a cab, if I have to carry him down to it."

"You will do nothing of the sort. You will persuade him to come. And then you will return in front of him. Make any excuse so as not to come with him. Don't forget, Watson. You won't fail me. You never did fail me. No doubt there are natural enemies which limit the increase of the creatures. You and I, Watson, we have done our part. Shall the world, then, be overrun by oysters? No, no; horrible! You'll convey all that is in your mind."

I left him full of the image of this magniˇcent intellect babbling like a foolish child. He had handed me the key, and with a happy thought I took it with me lest he should lock himself in. Mrs. Hudson was waiting, trembling and weeping, in the passage. Behind me as I passed from the at I heard Holmes's high, thin voice in some delirious chant. Below, as I stood whistling for a cab, a man came on me through the fog.

"How is Mr. Holmes, sir?" he asked.

It was an old acquaintance, Inspector Morton, of Scotland Yard, dressed in uncial tweeds.

"He is very ill," I answered.

He looked at me in a most singular fashion. Had it not been too fiendish, I could have imagined that the gleam of the fanlight showed exultation in his face.

"I heard some rumour of it," said he.

The cab had driven up, and I left him.

Lower Burke Street proved to be a line of fine houses lying in the vague borderland between Notting Hill and Kensington. The particular one at which my cabman pulled up had an air of smug and demure respectability in its old-fashioned iron railings, its massive folding-door, and its shining brasswork. All was in keeping with a solemn butler who ap- peared framed in the pink radiance of a tinted electrical light behind him.

"Yes, Mr. Culverton Smith is in. Dr. Watson! Very good, sir, I will take up your card."

My humble name and title did not appear to impress Mr. Culverton Smith. Through the half-open door I heard a high, petulant, penetrating voice.

"Who is this person? What does he want? Dear me, Staples, how often have I said that

I am not to be disturbed in my hours of study?"

There came a gentle ow of soothing explanation from the butler.

"Well, I won't see him, Staples. I can't have my work interrupted like this. I am not at home. Say so. Tell him to come in the morning if he really must see me."

Again the gentle murmur.

"Well, well, give him that message. He can come in the morning, or he can stay away.

My work must not be hindered."

I thought of Holmes tossing upon his bed of sickness and counting the minutes, perhaps, until I could bring help to him. It was not a time to stand upon ceremony. His life depended upon my promptness. Before the apologetic butler had delivered his message I had pushed past him and was in the room.

With a shrill cry of anger a man rose from a reclining chair beside the fire. I saw a great yellow face, coarse-grained and greasy, with heavy, double-chin, and two sullen, menacing gray eyes which glared at me from under tufted and sandy brows. A high bald head had a small velvet smoking-cap poised coquettishly upon one side of its pink curve. The skull was of enormous capacity, and yet as I looked down I saw to my amazement that the figure of the man was small and frail, twisted in the shoulders and back like one who has su"ered from rickets in his childhood.

"What's this?" he cried in a high, screaming voice. "What is the meaning of this intru- sion? Didn't I send you word that I would see you to-morrow morning?"

"I am sorry," said I, "but the matter cannot be delayed. Mr. Sherlock Holmes-"

The mention of my friend's name had an extraordinary e"ect upon the little man. The look of anger passed in an instant from his face. His features became tense and alert.

"Have you come from Holmes?" he asked.

"I have just left him."

"What about Holmes? How is he?"

"He is desperately ill. That is why I have come."

The man motioned me to a chair, and turned to resume his own. As he did so I caught a glimpse of his face in the mirror over the mantelpiece. I could have sworn that it was set in a malicious and abominable smile. Yet I persuaded myself that it must have been some nervous contraction which I had surprised, for he turned to me an instant later with genuine concern upon his features.

"I am sorry to hear this," said he. "I only know Mr. Holmes through some business dealings which we have had, but I have every respect for his talents and his character. He is an amateur of crime, as I am of disease. For him the villain, for me the microbe. There are my prisons," he continued, pointing to a row of bottles and jars which stood upon a side table. "Among those gelatine cultivations some of the very worst o"enders in the world are now doing time."

"It was on account of your special knowledge that Mr. Holmes desired to see you. He has a high opinion of you and thought that you were the one man in London who could help him."

The little man started, and the jaunty smoking-cap slid to the oor.

"Why?" he asked. "Why should Mr. Homes think that I could help him in his trouble?"

"Because of your knowledge of Eastern diseases."

"But why should he think that this disease which he has contracted is Eastern?"

"Because, in some professional inquiry, he has been working among Chinese sailors down in the docks."

Mr. Culverton Smith smiled pleasantly and picked up his smoking-cap.

"Oh, that's it{is it?" said he. "I trust the matter is not so grave as you suppose. How long has he been ill?"

"About three days."

"Is he delirious?"

"Occasionally."

"Tut, tut! This sounds serious. It would be inhuman not to answer his call. I very much resent any interruption to my work, Dr. Watson, but this case is certainly exceptional. I will come with you at once."

I remembered Holmes's injunction.

"I have another appointment," said I.

"Very good. I will go alone. I have a note of Mr. Holmes's address. You can rely upon my being there within half an hour at most."

It was with a sinking heart that I reentered Holmes's bedroom. For all that I knew the worst might have happened in my absence. To my enormous relief, he had improved greatly in the interval. His appearance was as ghastly as ever, but all trace of delirium had left him and he spoke in a feeble voice, it is true, but with even more than his usual crispness and lucidity.

"Well, did you see him, Watson?"

"Yes; he is coming."

"Admirable, Watson! Admirable! You are the best of messengers."

"He wished to return with me."

"That would never do, Watson. That would be obviously impossible. Did he ask what ailed me?"

"I told him about the Chinese in the East End."

"Exactly! Well, Watson, you have done all that a good friend could. You can now dis- appear from the scene."

"I must wait and hear his opinion, Holmes."

"Of course you must. But I have reasons to suppose that this opinion would be very much more frank and valuable if he imagines that we are alone. There is just room behind the head of my bed, Watson."

"My dear Holmes!"

"I fear there is no alternative, Watson. The room does not lend itself to concealment, which is as well, as it is the less likely to arouse suspicion. But just there, Watson, I fancy that it could be done." Suddenly he sat up with a rigid intentness upon his haggard face. "There are the wheels, Watson. Quick, man, if you love me! And don't budge, whatever happens{whatever happens, do you hear? Don't speak! Don't move! Just listen with all your ears." Then in an instant his sudden access of strength departed, and his masterful, purposeful talk droned away into the low, vague murmurings of a semi-delirious man.

From the hiding-place into which I had been so swiftly hustled I heard the footfalls upon the stair, with the opening and the closing of the bedroom door. Then, to my surprise, there came a long silence, broken only by the heavy breathings and gaspings of the sick man. I could imagine that our visitor was standing by the bedside and looking down at the su"erer. At last that strange hush was broken.

"Holmes!" he cried. "Holmes!" in the insistent tone of one who awakens a sleeper. "Can't you hear me, Holmes?" There was a rustling, as if he had shaken the sick man roughly by the shoulder.

"Is that you, Mr. Smith?" Holmes whispered. "I hardly dared hope that you would come."

The other laughed.

"I should imagine not," he said. "And yet, you see, I am here. Coals of ˇre, Holmes-coals of fire!"

"It is very good of you{very noble of you. I appreciate your special knowledge."

Our visitor sniggered.

"You do. You are, fortunately, the only man in London who does. Do you know what is the matter with you?"

"The same," said Holmes.

"Ah! You recognize the symptoms?"

"Only too well."

"Well, I shouldn't be surprised, Holmes. I shouldn't be surprised if it WERE the same. A bad lookout for you if it is. Poor Victor was a dead man on the fourth day{a strong, hearty young fellow. It was certainly, as you said, very surprising that he should have contracted an out-of-the-way Asiatic disease in the heart of London{a disease, too, of which I had made such a very special study. Singular coincidence, Holmes. Very smart of you to notice it, but rather uncharitable to suggest that it was cause and effect."

"I knew that you did it."

"Oh, you did, did you? Well, you couldn't prove it, anyhow. But what do you think of yourself spreading reports about me like that, and then crawling to me for help the moment you are in trouble? What sort of a game is that-eh?"

I heard the rasping, laboured breathing of the sick man. "Give me the water!" he gasped.

"You're precious near your end, my friend, but I don't want you to go till I have had a word with you. That's why I give you water. There, don't slop it about! That's right. Can you understand what I say?"

Holmes groaned.

"Do what you can for me. Let bygones be bygones," he whispered. "I'll put the words out of my head{I swear I will. Only cure me, and I'll forget it."

"Forget what?"

"Well, about Victor Savage's death. You as good as admitted just now that you had done it. I'll forget it."

"You can forget it or remember it, just as you like. I don't see you in the witnessbox. Quite another shaped box, my good Holmes, I assure you. It matters nothing to me that you should know how my nephew died. It's not him we are talking about. It's you."

"Yes, yes."

"The fellow who came for me{I've forgotten his name{said that you contracted it down in the East End among the sailors."

"I could only account for it so."

"You are proud of your brains, Holmes, are you not? Think yourself smart, don't you?

You came across someone who was smarter this time. Now cast your mind back, Holmes. Can you think of no other way you could have got this thing?"

"I can't think. My mind is gone. For heaven's sake help me!"

"Yes, I will help you. I'll help you to understand just where you are and how you got there. I'd like you to know before you die."

"Give me something to ease my pain."

"Painful, is it? Yes, the coolies used to do some squealing towards the end. Takes you as cramp, I fancy."

"Yes, yes; it is cramp."

"Well, you can hear what I say, anyhow. Listen now! Can you remember any unusual incident in your life just about the time your symptoms began?"

"No, no; nothing."

"Think again."

"I'm too ill to think."

"Well, then, I'll help you. Did anything come by post?"

"By post?"

"A box by chance?"

"I'm fainting{I'm gone!"

"Listen, Holmes!" There was a sound as if he was shaking the dying man, and it was all that I could do to hold myself quiet in my hiding-place. "You must hear me. You SHALL hear me. Do you remember a box{an ivory box? It came on Wednesday. You opened it-do you remember?"

"Yes, yes, I opened it. There was a sharp spring inside it. Some joke{"

"It was no joke, as you will find to your cost. You fool, you would have it and you have got it. Who asked you to cross my path? If you had left me alone I would not have hurt you."

"I remember," Holmes gasped. "The spring! It drew blood. This box{this on the table."

"The very one, by George! And it may as well leave the room in my pocket. There goes your last shred of evidence. But you have the truth now, Holmes, and you can die with the knowledge that I killed you. You knew too much of the fate of Victor Savage, so I have sent you to share it. You are very near your end, Holmes. I will sit here and I will watch you die."

Holmes's voice had sunk to an almost inaudible whisper.

"What is that?" said Smith. "Turn up the gas? Ah, the shadows begin to fall, do they?

Yes, I will turn it up, that I may see you the better." He crossed the room and the light suddenly brightened. "Is there any other little service that I can do you, my friend?"

"A match and a cigarette."

I nearly called out in my joy and my amazement. He was speaking in his natural voice{a little weak, perhaps, but the very voice I knew. There was a long pause, and I felt that

Culverton Smith was standing in silent amazement looking down at his companion.

"What's the meaning of this?" I heard him say at last in a dry, rasping tone.

"The best way of successfully acting a part is to be it," said Holmes. "I give you my word that for three days I have tasted neither food nor drink until you were good enough to pour me out that glass of water. But it is the tobacco which I ˇnd most irksome. Ah, here ARE some cigarettes." I heard the striking of a match. "That is very much better. Halloa! halloa! Do I hear the step of a friend?"

There were footfalls outside, the door opened, and Inspector Morton appeared.

"All is in order and this is your man," said Holmes.

The offcer gave the usual cautions.

"I arrest you on the charge of the murder of one Victor Savage," he concluded.

"And you might add of the attempted murder of one Sherlock Holmes," remarked my friend with a chuckle. "To save an invalid trouble, Inspector, Mr. Culverton Smith was good enough to give our signal by turning up the gas. By the way, the prisoner has a small box in the right-hand pocket of his coat which it would be as well to remove. Thank you. I would handle it gingerly if I were you. Put it down here. It may play its part in the trial."

There was a sudden rush and a scu/e, followed by the clash of iron and a cry of pain.

"You'll only get yourself hurt," said the inspector. "Stand still, will you?" There was the click of the closing handcu"s.

"A nice trap!" cried the high, snarling voice. "It will bring YOU into the dock, Holmes, not me. He asked me to come here to cure him. I was sorry for him and I came. Now he will pretend, no doubt, that I have said anything which he may invent which will corroborate his insane suspicions. You can lie as you like, Holmes. My word is always as good as yours."

"Good heavens!" cried Holmes. "I had totally forgotten him. My dear Watson, I owe you a thousand apologies. To think that I should have overlooked you! I need not introduce you to Mr. Culverton Smith, since I understand that you met somewhat earlier in the evening. Have you the cab below? I will follow you when I am dressed, for I may be of some use at the station.

"I never needed it more," said Holmes as he refreshed himself with a glass of claret and some biscuits in the intervals of his toilet. "However, as you know, my habits are irregular, and such a feat means less to me than to most men. It was very essential that I should impress Mrs. Hudson with the reality of my condition, since she was to convey it to you, and you in turn to him. You won't be o"ended, Watson? You will realize that among your many talents dissimulation ˇnds no place, and that if you had shared my secret you would never have been able to impress Smith with the urgent necessity of his presence, which was the vital point of the whole scheme. Knowing his vindictive nature, I was perfectly certain that he would come to look upon his handiwork."

"But your appearance, Holmes-your ghastly face?"

"Three days of absolute fast does not improve one's beauty, Watson. For the rest, there is nothing which a sponge may not cure. With vaseline upon one's forehead, belladonna in one's eyes, rouge over the cheek-bones, and crusts of beeswax round one's lips, a very satisfying e"ect can be produced.

Malingering is a subject upon which I have sometimes thought of writing a monograph. A little occasional talk about half-crowns, oysters, or any other extraneous subject produces a pleasing e"ect of delirium."

"But why would you not let me near you, since there was in truth no infection?"

"Can you ask, my dear Watson? Do you imagine that I have no respect for your medical talents? Could I fancy that your astute judgment would pass a dying man who, however weak, had no rise of pulse or temperature? At four yards, I could deceive you. If I failed to do so, who would bring my Smith within my grasp? No, Watson, I would not touch that box. You can just see if you look at it sideways where the sharp spring like a viper's tooth emerges as you open it. I dare say it was by some such device that poor Savage, who stood between this monster and a reversion, was done to death. My correspondence, however, is, as you know, a varied one, and I am somewhat upon my guard against any packages which reach me. It was clear to me, however, that by pretending that he had really succeeded in his design I might surprise a confession. That pretence I have carried out with the thoroughness of the true artist. Thank you, Watson, you must help me on with my coat. When we have finished at the police-station I think that something nutritious at Simpson's would not be out of place."